Jasper John Dooley
Lost and Found

Written by Caroline Adderson

Illustrated by Mike Shiell

Kids Can Press

For the little girl who lost her Topo Gigio — C.A.

Text © 2015 Caroline Adderson
Illustrations © 2015 Kids Can Press

Kids Can Press acknowledges the financial support of the Government of Ontario, through the Ontario Media Development Corporation's Ontario Book Initiative; the Ontario Arts Council; the Canada Council for the Arts; and the Government of Canada, through the CBF, for our publishing activity.

Published in Canada by	Published in the U.S. by
Kids Can Press Ltd.	Kids Can Press Ltd.
25 Dockside Drive	2250 Military Road
Toronto, ON M5A 0B5	Tonawanda, NY 14150

www.kidscanpress.com

Edited by Yasemin Uçar
Series designed by Rachel Di Salle
Designed by Julia Naimska
Illustrations by Mike Shiell, based on illustrations in Jasper John Dooley, Books 1–4 by Ben Clanton

This book is smyth sewn casebound.
Manufactured in Shen Zhen, Guang Dong, P.R. China, in 03/2015 by Printplus Limited

CM 15 0 9 8 7 6 5 4 3 2 1

Library and Archives Canada Cataloguing in Publication

Adderson, Caroline, author
    Jasper John Dooley, lost and found / written by Caroline Adderson ; illustrated by Mike Shiell.

(Jasper John Dooley ; 5)
ISBN 978-1-77138-014-0 (bound)

    I. Shiell, Mike, illustrator II. Title. III. Series: Adderson, Caroline, 1963– .
Jasper John Dooley ; 5.

PS8551.D3267L67 2015   jC813'.54   C2014-907192-2

Kids Can Press is a **C◯RUS**™ Entertainment company

Jasper John Dooley
Lost and Found

Contents

Chapter 1

At recess, Jasper John Dooley and Ori invented a new game. They were tired of knights and hide-and-seek. They really didn't want to play babies with the girls. The girls made them lie in the grass and wa-wa-wa and pretend to eat pinecones.

Today they were treasure hunters.

Jasper and Ori knelt in the sand near the jungle gym and dug. The deeper they dug, the harder it was. Jasper grabbed a plastic snack container lying on the ground. He used it to dig and gave Ori the lid.

"I found something!" Ori called out.

Jasper peered into Ori's hole. Something glinted at the bottom.

"Treasure!"

Both boys attacked the hole with their hands. Sand flew all around them until Ori pulled the treasure out.

"A bottle cap," he said, and slumped. "I thought it was gold."

They went back to digging. Jasper found a worm. It nearly got cut in half! Jasper carried the worm over to the bushes and hid it under some leaves, where it would be safe from birds *and* treasure hunters.

When he got back to his hole, Isabel and Zoë were standing over Ori with their hands on their hips.

"What are you doing, Ori?" Zoë asked.

"Digging for treasure."

"What kind of treasure?"

"Gold," Ori said. "Or silver."

"Ha ha ha!" Isabel laughed.

Jasper asked her to move because her foot was almost in his hole.

"You're never going to find treasure here," Isabel told him.

Jasper pretended the girls weren't there, but ignoring girls was the best way to interest them. They bent over, watching Jasper and Ori dig, ooh-ing when Jasper hit something hard, then giggling when he lifted a rock out of the hole.

"Jasper John," Isabel said, "if you're looking for treasure, I have some in my cubby."

Jasper stopped digging and looked up at Isabel.

She smiled, showing the empty front-tooth space in her mouth.

"What kind of treasure?" Jasper asked.

"I'll show you," Isabel said just as the bell rang.

Jasper and Ori followed Isabel and Zoë into the school. In the classroom, Isabel led them to her cubby, where her backpack was hanging on a hook. She unzipped the front pocket and reached inside it.

Ori gasped when he saw what Isabel took out.

Money. So so so much money!

"Treasure!" Ori exclaimed.

"Where did you get it?" Jasper asked Isabel.

"From the bowl in my front hall beside the phone," Isabel said.

Isabel had an idea for a game. A good one! At lunch she and Zoë would go ahead and bury the treasure. Then Jasper and Ori would dig for it.

"Whatever you find, you can keep," Isabel told them.

"Really?" Jasper said.

Isabel nodded. Jasper and Ori looked at each other.

"The thing is," Ori said, "we'll be rich."

So at lunch Jasper and Ori ended up playing with

Isabel and Zoë even though they hadn't wanted to. At least it wasn't babies!

First they stood on the school steps with their backs turned and counted to one hundred. That way the girls had enough time to bury the treasure. Then they tore down to the jungle gym. They dug and dug with the plastic container and the lid until the sand around the jungle gym was all holey.

Isabel and Zoë stood by, calling, "Not there!" and "Not even close!" and "Try again!"

When Jasper stopped to rest, he looked over at the girls. Their mouths got small like they were sucking on a peppermint. A peppermint or a joke. They glanced at each other and smiled.

By the time the after-lunch bell rang, Jasper and Ori weren't any richer.

Chapter 2

Every Wednesday, Jasper visited his Nan in her apartment not far from his house. They had fun riding the elevator up and down, making horrible faces in the mirrors on the walls, and playing Go Fish for jujubes and Dress Up Nan.

Today making a horrible face in the elevator mirror was easy. Jasper only had to think about digging holes while Isabel and Zoë tried not to laugh.

"Is that a *real* horrible face?" Nan asked.

"This face is for Isabel and Zoë, who tricked us!" Jasper told her.

Jasper told Nan the story. When he said, "I bet they didn't even bury that treasure!" Nan made a *real* horrible face, too.

The elevator stopped on Nan's floor and they got out. Jasper raced ahead to her door and rapped the jaws of the lion's head knocker even though Nan wasn't inside to answer.

"Too bad about the treasure," the lion said to Jasper in his liony voice.

"I know!" Jasper said back. "I wish I had some treasure to bury."

Nan unlocked the door for Jasper. "You're in luck. I just found a whole box of treasure. It's on the table."

"Really?" Jasper said.

He pulled off his shoes without undoing the laces and ran ahead to the kitchen. There was a box on the table, just like Nan said, with a string tied around it. The sort of box Mom liked — long and flat. Dad always gave her a box like this for her birthday, with a fancy nightie in it, except for the time he gave her a bigger box with a Dustbuster in it, and she got mad. Now Dad always gave her presents in boxes that were too long and flat to hold cleaning things.

Jasper jiggled the box. It was heavy, and the things inside rattled and slid. A word was written on the side: *TOYS*.

Nan sat at the table with Jasper. "I was down in the storage room this morning. I found it tucked away there."

"It's toys, not treasure," Jasper said.

"Small toys, if I remember right. They'll be perfect for burying and digging up. Open it."

"Toys!" Jasper crowed when they finally got the knot on the string undone and the lid lifted off. Lots and lots of little toys! Most of them were soldiers, but they were the funniest toy soldiers Jasper had ever seen.

"These soldiers are pink!" Jasper laughed.

"They were Tom's, back when he was about your age," Nan said.

Tom was Jasper's uncle. Jasper didn't see him very often because he lived far away in Australia.

"But your father? One day he took my nail polish and painted them."

"I know," Jasper said. "Dad told me. What did Uncle Tom do when he saw his soldiers were pink?"

"Oh, he was mad!"

Both of them started to laugh. They laughed so hard Jasper had to fetch Nan a tissue.

"What else is in there?" Nan asked Jasper when she had wiped her eyes.

"Marbles. Hockey cards," Jasper said. "And old-fashioned cars!"

"I guess they are old-fashioned now." Nan peered in the box. "And look! Oh, my goodness! This sure brings back memories!"

Out of the jumble of little toys, she plucked something orange and made of plastic. Something with big ears and big feet.

"Marcel Mouse," Nan said. "There was a TV show about this mouse. Tom and David would race home after school to watch it. They'd burst through the door, singing the jingle."

"What's a jingle?"

"The theme song for the show."

"Sing the song."

"I don't remember it, Jasper. But I remember those two little boys bursting into the house, singing. And I remember that Tom got Marcel Mouse as a prize in a box of popcorn. Your dad almost died of jealousy. He begged and pleaded for that mouse. In the end, I think he traded every toy he owned for it. Do you see this little loop between Marcel's ears? Your dad hung Marcel on a string around his neck and never took him off, not even in the bath."

"He loved Marcel Mouse," Jasper said.

Nan nodded.

"Then Marcel Mouse really *is* a treasure. But I'm never going to bury him."

Jasper took the string that had been tied around the box and threaded it through the loop between Marcel Mouse's big ears. With the two ends of the string, he tied a knot and hung the little orange mouse around his neck.

Marcel Mouse's string was long. It was so long that Marcel hung down by Jasper's belly button. Nan suggested he cut the string shorter, but Jasper said, "No. Marcel likes it so so long like this. On a so so long string, Marcel swings more. He has more fun."

Jasper shifted from foot to foot. This made Marcel swing out to each side. Marcel swung higher and higher until he was at shoulder level.

Nan watched him from the stove, where she was making macaroni. "I hope Marcel doesn't have motion sickness."

"What's that?"

"Some people feel like throwing up on boats or cars or rides at the fair."

"Marcel doesn't feel like throwing up. He loves it! Wheee!"

After supper, when Mom came to pick up Jasper, he showed her how Marcel Mouse could swing. Then they hugged Nan good-bye and left with Marcel and the box of treasure.

At home, Jasper burst into the living room, where Dad was lying on the sofa watching golf on TV. Jasper wished he knew the Marcel Mouse song. If he'd known it, he would have burst in singing it like Dad had when he was a boy.

Jasper stood in front of Dad with Marcel Mouse hanging down by his belly button.

"Hi, Jasper," Dad said.

Jasper smiled. "Hi."

Dad leaned to the side to see past Jasper. Jasper stepped in the way again.

"What are you doing, Jasper?" Dad asked.

"Showing you something."

Dad didn't notice Marcel Mouse because he was looking at Jasper's smiling face. "What?"

Jasper stuck out his tummy. Dad's eyes traveled down the string, all the way to the little plastic mouse with the big ears and big feet. He sat up straight.

"Is that *Marcel Mouse*?"

Jasper was surprised by what Dad did next — he sprang to his feet and began to sing: "*Marcel Mouse! Marcel Mouse! A mouse who's lots of fun! Marcel Mouse! Marcel Mouse! He's a tricky one!*"

Dad waved his hands high. He waved them low. He turned in a circle, waving his hands and singing.

"*Marcel Mouse!*" Jasper joined in. "*Marcel Mouse!*"

He sang and danced and waved high and low with Dad.

"That was my favorite show, Jasper," Dad said. "Every day Marcel got in trouble and every day he got out again. Once he got caught in a mousetrap. He held it open with his two skinny mouse arms, then with his tail performed the most amazing trick. He bent the wires of the trap and flipped it over. And you know what that trap became?"

"What?"

"A lawn chair!"

Dad threw himself on the sofa with his arms folded behind his head and one leg crossed over the other, his toe tapping the air. He looked just like he was sunning himself in a lawn chair. Jasper lay on the floor and sunned himself, too.

Dad looked down at Jasper. "Nan had Marcel?"

Jasper nodded.

"Let me wear him."

"No," Jasper said.

"Just for a little while."

"No. Nan gave him to me. He's mine."

"Come on." Dad reached for Marcel. Jasper clutched the little mouse to his chest, so Dad started tickling Jasper. Jasper laughed and squirmed, holding Marcel Mouse tight.

"You're just like Tom!" Dad said. "He wouldn't let me play with Marcel either." As soon as Dad mentioned Uncle Tom, he remembered something and sat up on the sofa. "Gail! Gail!"

Mom came to the living room with a big cookbook in her hands.

"Tom called," Dad told her. "He's coming for Mom's party."

"Really? He's coming for Nan's birthday? That's great!" Mom said.

"Uncle Tom's coming here?" Jasper jumped up and shouted, "Hurray!"

That night Jasper took a bath with Marcel Mouse the way Dad had when he was a little boy. Marcel headed out in a boat. Good thing he didn't have motion sickness, because right away the seas got stormy. Luckily, Marcel was attached to the so so long string. When the boat capsized in the middle of the ocean, Jasper pulled him back to land.

After his bath, Jasper climbed into bed with Marcel still hanging from the string around his neck. But Mom said he couldn't sleep wearing Marcel Mouse.

"When Dad was a little boy the same age as me,

Nan let him sleep with Marcel Mouse. Dad never took Marcel off," Jasper told her.

Mom said, "Nan is lucky her little boy didn't strangle on the string while he was asleep."

She said it was Very Dangerous to sleep with a plastic mouse on a string around his neck, and Jasper had to take Marcel off.

Jasper wrapped the wet string around and around Marcel's orange body until he looked like a mummy with his head sticking out. "Goodnight, Marcel," he said, looking into the orange mouse's surprised eyes. "I'll be right here."

He tucked Marcel under the pillow, patted it, then fell asleep humming the Marcel Mouse song.

Chapter 3

In the morning, the first thing Jasper did was slide his hand under the pillow.

"DAD!!!!"

Dad came running.

"Marcel Mouse is gone! Did you take him?"

"No," Dad said.

"You didn't sneak in and take him?"

Dad said, "I didn't. Honest."

"You tried to take him from Uncle Tom."

"I *traded* for him," Dad said. "You're the only one in this family who sneaks into bedrooms when people are sleeping and *steals.*"

Steals belly button lint, he meant. Sometimes Jasper snuck into Mom and Dad's room early in the morning to do this.

"Marcel's got to be here somewhere," Dad said. "Let's look."

Jasper threw off the covers. He and Dad got down on their hands and knees and looked under the bed. "What are those big blobs?" Jasper asked.

"Dust bunnies. I'll get the broom."

Dad came back with the broom and swept all the dust bunnies out from under the bed. They looked like lint clouds. Other things were mingled with the bunnies.

"My yo-yo," Jasper said. "And there's the gold pencil crayon Mrs. Kinoshita gave me."

"And there's an apple core, a scrunchy tissue and some very dusty underpants," Dad said. "And look, Jasper. Over in the corner. An empty wastebasket."

Jasper didn't laugh. "But where's Marcel? Marcel is lost!"

"You get dressed, Jasper. I'll keep looking."

"Let's sing the song," Jasper said. "He might be hiding. He might be afraid to come out because he's in a new place."

"Marcel isn't the kind of mouse to be afraid. But sure. Let's sing."

And it worked! While Jasper was dressing and he and Dad were singing, *Marcel Mouse! Marcel Mouse! A mouse who's lots of fun!,* Dad found

Marcel jammed between Jasper's mattress and the headboard.

Jasper lunged for Marcel and snatched him from Dad.

"I know you," Jasper told Dad. "You're a tricky one."

Jasper got the lates. He got the lates because Marcel was lost, then found, and because all the way to school he and Dad sang the Marcel Mouse song at the top of their lungs and danced the dance. It was slower dancing to school than walking because some of the dance was turning in a circle.

When Jasper came into the classroom, he stopped to explain to everybody why he'd got the lates. He showed them Marcel Mouse hanging around his neck.

"My Nan found Marcel in a box in her storage room. He used to be my dad's mouse. My dad even slept with him. He's lucky that he never strangled on Marcel's string."

Ms. Tosh said, "Jasper? Bernadette is the Star this week. She presented her Show and Tell on Monday."

"I'm just explaining why I got the lates."

Ms. Tosh told him to sit down. "You can tell everybody about your mouse at recess."

Jasper sat down at his table. Now he wished he'd made the so so long string longer. If it had been just a bit longer, if it had been so so *so* long, Marcel would reach the chair and be sitting, too.

Instead, Jasper stood him up on the table. Margo, who sat next to Jasper, leaned over to look at Marcel. "He's so cute!" she said.

Ori, at the next table, leaned across the aisle to get a better look at Marcel. The two kids who sat in front of Jasper — Leon and Paul C.— turned in their seats to look, too.

"Jasper John Dooley," Ms. Tosh called, "put that mouse away."

Good thing the string was so so long! Marcel could be in the book slot under the table and still hang from the string around Jasper's neck.

When the bell rang for recess, everybody followed Jasper outside so they could meet Marcel. They lined up. With Marcel still hanging on the string around his neck, Jasper let everybody touch him. Some of the girls kissed Marcel. Some of the boys kissed him, too. When Ori got to the front of the line, Jasper whispered, "I'll let you wear him after school."

Then Jasper taught all the kids the Marcel Mouse song and dance. Some kids who weren't even in their class saw what they were doing and ran over to join in. After they had sung the song and danced the dance, they formed a big circle around Jasper so he could show them how Marcel could fly. Jasper shifted from foot to foot. Marcel swung higher and higher until he was level with Jasper's shoulders.

Then Jasper planted his feet and moved his upper body in a circle like he was Hula-hooping.

Marcel took off. Around and around Jasper's neck, at the end of the so so long string, Marcel soared.

"I want to try!" Leon yelled.

He stepped forward and — *smack*! Marcel flew right into Leon.

"OWWW!!!!!"

Leon fell to his knees holding the side of his head. Jasper crouched beside him. "Sorry, Leon." He stood Marcel on Leon's shoulder and made him squeak that he was sorry, too.

The playground monitor arrived just as the bell rang. Everybody went back to the classroom except for Leon and Jasper and Marcel, who went to the principal's office.

"*Marcel Mouse! Marcel Mouse! A mouse who's lots of fun! Marcel Mouse! Marcel Mouse! He's a tricky one!*"

Jasper waved his hands high. He waved them low. He turned in a circle, waving his hands and singing.

"Jasper?" Mrs. Kinoshita said.

Jasper stopped singing and dancing and waving because he had to. Mrs. Kinoshita was the principal.

She pointed to the big chair across from her desk. Jasper didn't like to sit there. It made him nervous because his feet didn't touch the ground. He said, "I found the gold pencil crayon you gave me. It was under my bed with some dust bunnies."

"Please sit down," Mrs. Kinoshita said.

"I need to show you how Marcel flies. So you know what happened to Leon."

Leon was okay. He'd already gone back to the classroom.

"Jasper? This is how you got in trouble in the first place."

Jasper nodded and said, "Every day Marcel gets in trouble. Every day he gets out again."

"It's better if Marcel doesn't get in trouble while he's at school. Either he stays in the office during school time or he stays home. Do you understand?"

"Marcel was my dad's mouse. He wore him all the time. He never took him off."

Mrs. Kinoshita folded her hands on the desk and looked at Jasper. She only had to look at him. She was the principal.

Jasper said, "Can he stay with you?"

"I'll leave him on Mrs. Jamil's desk."

Jasper didn't want to, but he lifted off the so so long string around his neck. He wrapped it around and around Marcel's orange plastic body until he looked like a little mouse mummy with his head sticking out. He peered in Marcel's orange, surprised eyes and said, "I'll come and get you after school. Don't get lost again."

Chapter 4

After school, Ori went out to meet Jasper's mom. She always walked them both home because Ori's mom was busy with Ori's baby sister. Jasper went to the office to pick up Marcel Mouse.

"A mouse?" said Mrs. Jamil. "On my desk?"

"Yes," Jasper told her. "Mrs. Kinoshita put him there. She says I can bring him to school as long as I leave him with you."

"This is the first I've heard about any mouse, Jasper. Come and see for yourself."

Jasper went around the big counter and looked at Mrs. Jamil's desk. He saw papers and a computer and a mug of pens and pencils. He didn't see Marcel Mouse. Mrs. Jamil even let Jasper look in the desk drawers. They were full of office assistant things, like paper clips and juggling balls and hand cream.

Jasper didn't panic the way he had that morning. He told Mrs. Jamil, "Marcel is a very tricky mouse. When he got lost this morning, we found him. All we have to do is sing the song."

"What song?"

"The Marcel Mouse song. It's easy. Sing with me."

When Mom and Ori came to the office looking for Jasper, they found him and Mrs. Jamil singing, *"Marcel Mouse! Marcel Mouse! A mouse who's lots of fun!*" Ori joined in right away because he knew the words, then Mom did.

Mrs. Jamil stopped singing. "Oh! Do you mean the little toy all wrapped up in dirty string?"

"Yes!" Jasper cried.

"I put him in the Lost and Found box. I didn't realize he was a mouse."

They all went out to the hall where the big Lost and Found box was. Jasper and Ori looked inside. It was half full, mostly with clothes. But right on top was a little orange mouse with big ears and surprised eyes, wrapped in a so so long string.

Jasper kissed Marcel. Ori kissed him. Mrs. Jamil took Marcel back to the office and dabbed his face with hand sanitizer. Then she kissed him, too.

"I have an idea. Just so this never happens again, let's leave Marcel in the sickroom from now on."

The sickroom was next to the office. Mrs. Jamil took a box of tissues from the cupboard there. She showed Jasper how Marcel could sleep inside the box, under a cozy tissue blanket, safe in the cupboard.

Jasper said, "Thank you!" And he unwound the string and hung Marcel around his neck again. Marcel swung. "Wheee!"

Mom and Ori and Jasper walked home. Jasper lived the closest to the school, just a block away.

Ori lived the second closest, across the alley and one house down from Jasper.

"I'm not surprised Marcel was hiding in the Lost and Found box," Jasper told Mom and Ori. "He was living in a box in Nan's storage room. He's used to it."

"Can I wear Marcel now?" Ori asked.

"Sorry! I forgot," Jasper said.

"That's nice of you, Jasper," Mom said.

"The thing is," Ori said, "Jasper promised me I could wear him on the way home."

Ori stopped at the alley. Before he walked to his own house, he tried to make Marcel swing, but couldn't.

"Don't worry," Jasper told him. "You can try again tomorrow."

Chapter 5

The next day, after dancing with Dad to school singing the Marcel Mouse song, Jasper stopped at the sickroom and tucked Marcel in his tissue-box bed. *"Marcel Mouse! Marcel Mouse!"* Jasper sang. *"Don't get lost today!"*

All the way to the classroom, he hummed the Marcel Mouse song under his breath. On the way to school, Dad had said, "The Marcel Mouse song is a very catchy tune. Everybody at work is humming it. Even Mom is humming it."

When Jasper got to the classroom, everybody was humming it there, too. While everybody was writing Compliments to Bernadette, the Star, and eating the special cupcake snack that she had brought, they sang the song under their breaths.

"Marcel Mouse! Marcel Mouse! He's a tricky one!"

At recess Jasper went to the sickroom to check on Marcel Mouse. He was sleeping.

"Is he still there?" Mrs. Jamil asked.

Jasper gave her the thumbs-up.

He met Ori, Leon and Paul C. outside.

"Let's dig for treasure," Ori said.

Treasure! Jasper had forgotten all about the treasure Nan had given him. "We'll never find treasure here," Jasper said. "Next week I'll bring a whole box of things that we can bury and dig up."

So they played hide-and-seek. Paul C. was It. He sat on the picnic table and took off his glasses. He didn't need to cover his eyes. Without his glasses, he couldn't see a thing.

While Paul C. counted loudly to ten, Leon ran to the bushes at the back of the schoolyard where the playground monitor couldn't see him. He thought that Paul C. wouldn't find him there either, even after he put his glasses back on. But that was everybody's favorite place to hide, so it was the first place Paul C. looked. Jasper, hiding under the picnic table, watched Paul C. tag Leon.

Leon was It.

Now Leon sat on the picnic table. He covered his eyes and shouted, "Marcel Mouse! Marcel Mouse! One, two, three, four, five!"

Paul C. crouched behind a garbage can. Jasper and Ori snuck into the school.

Usually they hid outside, but hiding outside was getting boring. Bushes, picnic table, garbage can, trees. Bushes, picnic table, garbage can, trees …

"Here!" Jasper said, stopping in the hall in front of the Lost and Found box.

Ori crouched next to it.

"No," Jasper said. "Inside."

Jasper lifted the lid and climbed into the box. He dug a hole in the clothes deep enough to make a little nest. That way the lid of the box wouldn't touch his head. "Come on," he told Ori. "There's lots of room."

Ori climbed in, too, and dug himself a nest. They closed the lid.

Inside, the box smelled of that special flowery lint

smell, the fabric-softener-clean-clothes-start-of-a-new-day smell that Jasper loved. And old cheese, which Jasper didn't love.

"Dark!" Ori said.

"Just think," Jasper said, "Marcel was in a dark box like this almost forever before I took him out."

They stopped talking because they heard footsteps near the box. Ori poked Jasper. "Stop humming."

"I'm not humming."

"You are. You're humming the Marcel Mouse song. If Leon walks by, he'll hear us."

A different tune chimed out then, but not from Jasper. Muffled and far away, it sounded like an ice-cream truck three streets over. It was coming from under them, from under all the lost clothes in the Lost and Found box. When the tune finished, they heard a soft *"Bleep!"*

"What was that?" Ori asked.

"A game," Jasper said. "Let's find it."

In the darkness of the box, through all the Lost clothes, they dug down. The game helped them. It went "*Bleep! Bleep! Bleep!*" which meant, "*You're getting closer!*"

Jasper's hand closed around the game. He pulled it out through the tunnel of Lost clothes. The game seemed happy to be rescued. It played its tune again and flashed its colored lights so Jasper could see Ori's face in the dark of the Lost and Found box. His eyes were wide.

"Wow!" Ori said.

And the lid of the box opened and daylight flooded in. A hand came down on Ori's head.

"You're It!" Leon hollered.

At lunch Jasper went to the sickroom to check on Marcel Mouse. He ended up staying so he could fly Marcel around and around his neck at the end of the so so long string.

Ori stood in the doorway so he wouldn't get smacked the way Leon had the day before. He asked Jasper, "Who do you think lost that game?"

Jasper said, "I don't know."

"What happens if nobody comes for it?"

"They give it away."

"Who to?"

"People."

"What people?"

"I don't know their names. They pack all the Lost and Found things in boxes and take them away. I saw them do it last year."

"Maybe I could borrow the game," Ori said.

Jasper said, "Wheee!" because Marcel was having so much fun flying in the sickroom.

"Would you borrow the game?" Ori asked Jasper.

"I don't need a game. I have Marcel Mouse! Marcel Mouse! A mouse who's lots of fun!"

"I don't have a mouse," Ori said.

"Then borrow the game."

"The thing is, I'm not allowed games that bleep."

Mrs. Jamil came back from lunch and found the boys in the sickroom. "Jasper, are you still here?

Go outside and play. You, too, Ori."

"I was just checking on Marcel. He was bored. He wanted to fly."

"Out, out!" she said.

By then, lunch was nearly over. They didn't have time for more hide-and-seek.

After lunch, when all the kids were back in the classroom, an announcement came over the intercom. It was Mrs. Kinoshita reminding everybody about the assembly on Monday.

"And Jasper John Dooley?" she added. "Marcel Mouse is doing fine."

Everybody, even Ms. Tosh, laughed.

Chapter 6

Jasper, Mom and Ori walked home after school. On the way, Mom asked, "Do you need to go to the bathroom, Jasper?"

Jasper said, "How did you know?"

"The thing is, moms always know," Ori said. He was wearing Marcel Mouse on the so so long string around his neck.

"I never know when *you* have to go," Jasper told Mom.

Mom laughed. "I guess I don't do a little dance."

"Was I dancing?" Jasper asked.

"Yes. And humming a song."

"Like this?" Jasper waved his hands high and low and turned in a circle. He hummed the Marcel Mouse song.

"Not quite," Mom said. "Hurry ahead if you need to."

"Then Ori won't get a whole turn with Marcel."

They all walked together, Jasper dancing and humming. He really needed to go. As soon as they reached the alley and Ori had hung Marcel back around Jasper's neck, Jasper took off running.

Jasper ran all the rest of the way home and up the back stairs. Luckily, Mom hadn't locked the door. He slipped out of his shoes without undoing the laces and raced to the bathroom. The toilet lid was down.

Mom had been the last person in the bathroom, Jasper could tell. If Dad or Jasper had been the last one to use the bathroom, the toilet seat and lid would be up.

Jasper was in such a hurry that he only lifted the lid, not the seat. Marcel Mouse got quite a view from where he hung down by Jasper's belly button. Marcel probably thought he was standing at the top of a waterfall!

Then a terrible thing happened.

Jasper leaned over to flush the toilet. When he leaned, Marcel Mouse swung forward on the so so long string around Jasper's neck. With Marcel dangling right above the toilet bowl, Jasper flushed. His hand knocked against the lid and it fell closed.

Crack! went the lid against the toilet seat.

Snap! went the so so long string around Jasper's neck.

Down, down, down went Marcel Mouse! *Down, down, down* the toilet!

"NOOOO!!!!!!" Jasper screamed.

"What happened?" Mom called from the front door. She ran all the way to the bathroom where Jasper had sunk onto the floor.

"Marcel's lost!" Jasper wailed. "He's lost forever!"

When Dad got home from work, Jasper was lying on the sofa with a cold cloth over his eyes. They were so so so puffy from crying. Dad sat on the sofa and put Jasper's head in his lap. He lifted the cloth and smiled at Jasper, but Jasper didn't smile back.

"Jasper John," Dad said, "tell me what happened."

"Marcel Mouse got flushed down the toilet. The lid fell just as I flushed. It snapped the string. Marcel's dead. He drowned."

Jasper felt his whole body start to shake with new sobs. But no tears came. He had dried up from so much crying.

"Look." Jasper pulled up his shirt to show Dad the two Band-Aids stuck in an *X* on the left side of his chest. "These Band-Aids are because my heart is broken."

"Now, Jasper," Dad said, "remember how I told you about Marcel Mouse's TV show?"

Jasper nodded.

"I'm going to tell you about one of my favorite episodes."

Jasper listened.

"Marcel was out on a boat when a storm blew up," Dad began.

"He doesn't get motion sickness," Jasper said.

"So you already know that."

"I know because he loves it when I swing him on the so so long string. He doesn't throw up."

Dad said, "The time that I'm telling you about? His boat actually sank. But Marcel's a tricky one. Quick, quick, he grabbed the cheese out of the cargo hold and shaped it into a ring."

"A life preserver?"

Dad sat back and looked at Jasper. "Jasper John, you astound me."

Mom had been listening in the doorway. She came and sat on the sofa, too, and put Jasper's feet in her lap.

"Was Marcel okay?" she asked.

"Marcel was not okay. The smell of the cheese and the smell of the mouse brought a shark."

"Oh, no!" Mom said. "What did he do?"

Dad said, "Oh, he's a tricky one! He stuffed cheese up the shark's nose!"

"Really?" Jasper said with a laugh.

"Really. And while the shark was thrashing around with its cheese-stuffed nose, that tricky mouse grabbed his suitcase, opened it like a boat and caught an ocean current. He washed up on a beautiful island where the mice wore grass skirts and played tiny mouse instruments."

"He didn't drown?"

"No," Dad said.

Jasper realized something then. "Dad! He can't drown. He's made of plastic. He floats."

"You're right, Jasper!" Mom said.

"So you see, Jasper? No matter what kind of trouble Marcel gets into, it always turns into an adventure. His show always ended the same way, with Marcel closing his suitcase and slapping a sticker on it. It was a sticker of the place he'd visited in the episode."

"You mean Marcel might not be lost?" Jasper asked. "You mean he might be on a trip?"

"That's what I think," Dad said. "What do you think, Jasper?"

Jasper sat up on the sofa and grinned. "I think you're right!"

Chapter 7

On Saturday after soccer, Mom suggested they go to the library. "Let's find out where Marcel Mouse is headed."

They got on their bikes and rode to the library. While Mom and Dad locked the bikes in the rack, Jasper went inside and over to the desk where the librarian sat like a hen in a nest. He told her the whole story.

"Marcel Mouse was my dad's mouse. He wore him on a string around his neck. He never took him off."

"Never?" the librarian asked, just as Dad joined them.

Jasper turned to Dad. "You *did* take him off. How else did he get in the box at Nan's?"

"I grew up, Jasper," Dad said.

"Until he grew up," Jasper told the librarian, "he always wore Marcel Mouse. Then my Nan put Marcel in a box and forgot all about him until last week when she found the box in her storage room. She gave Marcel to me and I never took him off either. Except when I went to bed, because it's Very Dangerous to wear a so so long string around your neck when you're asleep."

The librarian nodded.

"And at school," Jasper said. "At school Marcel napped in a tissue box in the sickroom."

"We're looking for an atlas," Dad told her.

The librarian said, "I'll help you in a minute, sir. This patron hasn't finished telling me his story."

Jasper had to whisper the song because you aren't supposed to sing in the library where people are reading. He did the dance, waving high and low and turning in a circle. Then he told her about the terrible thing that had happened.

"Flushed down the toilet!" The librarian shook her head and clucked her tongue, just like a hen. Then she came out from behind her desk and led them to the shelf where the atlases were.

An atlas is a book of maps. They took down the biggest one. When they opened it, Jasper remembered something.

"We have an atlas at home," he said.

"A small one," Dad said. "We need one big enough

to figure out where Marcel is headed. We need one that shows the ocean currents."

Mom came over with some cookbooks. She needed more recipes for Nan's party. They sat together at a table and turned the pages of the atlas until they found a picture of the whole world. In the blue parts of the picture, the ocean parts, arrows showed which way the oceans flowed.

"According to this," Mom said, "Marcel could be heading to Alaska."

"Alaska!" Jasper said. "Nan went to Alaska!"

"If Marcel is lucky, he might even catch a ride on a cruise ship," Dad said.

Jasper had gone to see Nan off when she left on her cruise. The ship was huge. It looked like an apartment building lying on its side, except it was white and it floated. It had a swimming pool, a ballroom and ten restaurants. Ten restaurants on one ship! Nan had told Jasper all about it.

"Marcel would have a lot of fun on a cruise ship," Jasper said.

Dad traced his finger on the map. "And from Alaska, it looks like the next place he'll end up is Japan."

Dad named other countries after that. Jasper hadn't even heard of some of the countries where Marcel Mouse was headed. But the last country he had heard about: Australia.

"Australia? That's where Uncle Tom lives! Do you think Marcel will see Uncle Tom?"

"Well, it's a big country," Mom said.

"But maybe he'll look up all the Dooleys in the phone book. Maybe he'll find Uncle Tom and ask him to bring him back."

Mom and Dad looked at each other. Then Dad said, "While we're here, I think we should find out exactly how a toilet works."

They went to find a book about toilets.

That night, instead of reading stories before bed, Jasper and Mom and Dad read the book about toilets. They learned all the parts of the toilet and how a toilet flushed. They saw pictures of toilets from other countries in the world. In Japan, they had toilets that squirted water like a fountain. They had toilets with heaters in the seats.

"Marcel is going to be so so so surprised if he makes it to Japan," Jasper said.

On Sunday morning, Jasper went over to Ori's house across the alley and one house down. He rang the doorbell, but nobody answered because of the wa-wa-wa coming from inside. It was Rachel, Ori's baby sister. They called her the Watermelon. That was what she looked like before she was born, like a watermelon stuffed under Ori's mom's shirt.

Jasper opened the door and called hello.

Ori's head popped out of the Watermelon's room. He said, "Come and help."

The baby was on the change table, kicking her legs and waving her fists and going wa-wa-wa. Ori and his dad were on either side, Ori holding her down, his dad wrestling with a diaper. It looked like they were trying to wrap a very angry birthday present.

"Why is she crying?" Jasper asked.

"She hates having her diaper changed," Ori said.

Ori's dad told the Watermelon, "Hold still. How can I get a clean one on you when you're squirming so much?"

Jasper came over and looked down at the Watermelon. He liked her little purple face and the way her tongue pushed back in her gummy mouth.

"Watermelon?" Jasper told her. "You know where

we're going this afternoon? To the sewage treatment plant!"

At the sound of Jasper's voice, the Watermelon stopped crying and lay still. She gazed up at Jasper with her big eyes.

"Do you know what a sewage treatment plant is, Watermelon? It's where all the dirty toilet water goes before it's allowed back into the ocean."

As quick as he could, Ori's dad folded the diaper around her, and he and Ori closed the tapes.

"You sure have a way with this baby, Jasper," Ori's dad said. He lifted the Watermelon off the change table. She smiled at Jasper.

"Why are you going to the sewage treatment plant?" Ori asked.

"Marcel Mouse got flushed down the toilet!"

"What?" Ori said.

"We think he's leaving on a trip. Do you want to come with us and see him off?"

"Where the dirty toilet water goes?" Ori wrinkled his nose and took a step backward. "The thing is, my mom's out, and I have to help look after the Watermelon."

"Take this," said Ori's dad, holding out the Watermelon's diaper.

"Yuck!"

Jasper ran away, back across the alley and one house down.

The drive to the sewage treatment plant was long. They stopped for ice cream on the way. When they finally arrived, they parked and got out of the car for a closer look. Jasper stuck his hands through the wire fence and stared at the big concrete building.

"What's treatment?" he asked.

"It means the water gets cleaned," Mom said. "So there aren't any germs."

"Marcel's face got washed with hand sanitizer," Jasper said.

"Similar," Mom said.

The building was enormous. It was the size of five schools. "Do you think he'll know how to get out?"

"I know he will," Dad said. "He's been through worse trouble than this. He's probably out already. Let's go look."

They got back in the car and drove for a few minutes until they came to a park by the ocean.

People were walking in the sunshine and throwing Frisbees to their dogs on the beach.

Jasper and Mom and Dad went for a walk, too, down a long, narrow road. It was the funniest road Jasper had ever seen because it was built on top of the water and it didn't go anywhere. No cars were allowed, just people and dogs and bikes. When they reached the end, Dad explained that under the road was a long, long pipe. Cleaned-up water from the sewage treatment plant flowed through the pipe and into the ocean.

"This is where Marcel Mouse will start his trip," Dad said.

They sat on the bench near the water and watched for something small and orange with big ears and big feet, trailing a so so long broken string. After a while,

they decided that Marcel Mouse had already caught
a current. He was already on his way to Alaska.

Jasper asked Mom for a tissue. She took one from
her purse and gave it to him. Jasper stood on the
bench and waved the tissue. *"Marcel Mouse!"* he sang.
"Marcel Mouse! Come home soon!"

Chapter 8

At school on Monday, Patty was the Star of the Week. It was hard for Jasper to focus on her Show and Tell. He wanted to tell everybody what had happened to Marcel.

Patty had brought a caterpillar that she kept in a glass jar with holes punched in the lid. Its name was Kitty Cat.

"I named my caterpillar Kitty Cat because I really want a kitten. But I'm allergic," she told the class.

She passed around the jar and everybody got a

chance to see Kitty Cat up close munching on the leaves in the jar. Kitty Cat was green.

Ms. Tosh asked if anybody had questions for Patty.

Paul C. asked, "If you had a cat, would you name it Caterpillar?"

Ori asked, "If you had a cat, would you feed it leaves?"

Jasper waved his hand around.

Ms. Tosh said, "Patty told us a lot of interesting things about caterpillars. Can anybody remember one of those interesting things? Jasper?"

Jasper was waving his hand so that he could tell the class that Marcel Mouse got flushed down the toilet. Now he had to tell Ms. Tosh an interesting thing about caterpillars. He didn't know any because he'd lost focus while Patty was talking. But he did know an interesting thing *not* about caterpillars.

"I know a so so so so so interesting thing," he said.

"Go ahead and tell us, Jasper."

"If you pour a cup of water into the toilet, the amount of water in the bowl will stay the same."

"Pardon me?" Ms. Tosh said.

"You can even pour two cups or three cups or four. You can pour three hundred cups of water into the toilet and the amount of water will stay the same."

Nobody said anything at first. Then they started to laugh. Everybody fell over their tables laughing. Some kids — Leon and Paul C. — fell right off their chairs and onto the floor. Ms. Tosh had to clap her hands to get them to settle down again.

"What does that have to do with caterpillars?" Ms. Tosh asked Jasper.

"Nothing."

"Is it true?" somebody shouted.

"Is it?" somebody else shouted.

"Is it? Is it? Is it?" everybody wanted to know.

"I'm not sure," Ms. Tosh said. "Should we do an experiment?"

Everybody, including Patty, shouted, "Yes!"

Ms. Tosh asked Patty to bring cups from the art station. They all marched down the hall in a neat line. When they got to the bathrooms, Ms. Tosh said, "Kids, we have a problem."

She pointed to the girl symbol on one door and the boy symbol on the other.

They talked together about the problem before deciding to separate into two groups. Ms. Tosh took the girls into their bathroom first. The boys waited in the hall.

While the girls were doing the toilet experiment with Ms. Tosh, the boys were supposed to stay in the neat line and not make noise. But Ori broke away and snuck over to the Lost and Found box. He opened the lid and rooted around inside.

"What's that?" Paul C. asked when Ori came back with the game that bleeped.

Ori showed him. He asked everybody, "Is this yours? Did you lose it?" Nobody had, so Ori said, "I'm borrowing it."

The boys clustered around Ori and the game. Ori turned it on and the game chimed its tune, then went, "*Bleep!*" Ori didn't know what to do next, but Leon did. He had the same game at home.

"Press this. Now choose a game. Now play."

"*Bleep! Bleep! Bleep! Bleep! Bleep!*" went the game.

When they heard the toilet flush, the boys fell back in line. Ori stuffed the game down his shirt. It looked like the start of a watermelon, except it was a rectangle.

Next the girls waited in the hall while Ms. Tosh took the boys into their bathroom to do the toilet experiment.

"Ms. Tosh?" Ori said. "The thing is, you're not a boy."

"That's a good point, Ori. But the janitor who cleans the bathroom at the end of the day isn't a boy either. Any sort of adult is allowed."

Ms. Tosh opened the stall door. All the boys checked the water level in the toilet bowl. Then, one by one, each boy went to the sink for a cup of water, came back and poured the water in. When Ori poured his water, the game under his shirt went, "*Bleep!*"

Ori jumped. He looked at Ms. Tosh, but she was busy making sure nobody spilled water on the floor.

No matter how much they poured in, the water level in the toilet stayed the same!

Ms. Tosh marched the boys out to join the girls waiting in the hall. They all marched back to the classroom. The whole way, everybody chattered excitedly about the magic toilet.

"It's not magic," Ms. Tosh said. But she couldn't explain it. "I'm going to look it up. And Jasper? How did you find out this interesting thing?"

Finally!

Jasper said, "Marcel Mouse got flushed away!"

Chapter 9

After Jasper told the class about Marcel Mouse getting flushed down the toilet, he started to feel all watery inside. He'd brought Nan's box of treasure to school to play treasure hunters, but now he didn't feel like it. He felt like lying on the cot in the sickroom with the box of tissues on his chest.

But Mrs. Jamil wouldn't let him. He had to go outside.

So Jasper and Ori and Paul C. went to find Isabel and Zoë. They were playing hopscotch at the front of the school.

Jasper held up the long, flat box. The things inside rattled and slid. "Look what we have. Treasure!"

The girls dropped their hopscotch stones and came over. "What kind of treasure?" Zoë asked.

"Toy treasure," Isabel said, reading the word on the side of the box.

From the expressions on their faces, Jasper could tell they were excited about the toys.

"We're going to bury this treasure," Paul C. told them. "At lunch, you can dig it up."

"Whatever you find, you can keep," Ori told them.

The girls' eyes got wide.

"Really?" they said.

The boys nodded, then looked at each other and smiled.

Isabel and Zoë promised not to peek while the

boys were burying the treasure. Just in case, Paul C. stood by the jungle gym with his arms crossed, watching for them. He even cleaned his glasses.

Jasper knelt in the sand and dug a deep hole with the plastic container. "When they find this treasure and see it's soldiers, they're going to be so so mad."

Ori dug with the lid. They each dropped a pink soldier in the hole they had dug and cackled as they buried it.

After lunch, Isabel and Zoë followed the boys down to the jungle gym. They brought spoons from their lunches to dig with. They dug and dug until the sand around the jungle gym was all holey.

Jasper and Ori and Paul C. stood by, calling, "Not there!" and "Not even close!" and "Try again!"

Finally Isabel hit something. "Treasure!" she shrieked.

The boys looked at each other, and their mouths got small like they were sucking on a big burst of laughter.

Isabel pulled the treasure out. "A soldier? A *pink* soldier?"

"I found one, too!" Zoë hollered a second later. "He's so cute!"

The girls studied each other's soldiers. Then Isabel said, "Let's dig up some more and have a battle!"

They brushed off the soldiers' pink, sandy faces, slipped them in their pockets, then dug again.

And the boys stomped back to the school.

After school, when Mom came to pick up Jasper and Ori, she told Jasper she had a surprise for him at home.

"He needs a surprise," Ori said, giving Jasper a pat on the back.

Jasper's shoulders slumped. His head hung low.

"What's wrong, Jasper?" Mom asked.

Jasper groaned and clutched his tummy where Marcel Mouse would be hanging if he hadn't flushed him down the toilet.

"First he lost Marcel. Now he lost all his pink soldiers," Ori explained.

"All of them?" Mom asked. "There were so many. How did that happen?"

"We said the girls could keep what they dug up," Ori told her. "They dug up all of them."

"I loved those pink soldiers!" Jasper wailed.

"The thing is, the girls love them, too."

"Won't they give any of them back?" Mom asked.

The boys shook their heads.

"I know," Mom said. "Why don't we sing the Marcel Mouse song? I'm singing it all day long anyway."

"Marcel is gone," Jasper sniffed. "All that's left of him is his song!"

"Singing the song will cheer you up. So will the surprise at home."

Mom was right. Singing cheered Jasper up. All three of them waved high and low and turned in a circle on the sidewalk and crashed into each other and almost fell down. When they crashed, a *bleep!* came from Ori's backpack.

"Can Jasper come over?" Ori asked Mom.

"Yes, but he has to come home for his surprise first. Remember?"

"Yeah!" Jasper said. He was ready for the surprise now.

When they got home, Jasper tore all through the house looking for the surprise. "It's here," Mom said, pointing to her computer.

She opened her email. Jasper saw the message right away. The heading was: HELLO, JASPER!

A picture of a ship popped up on the screen. The ship was so big it looked like an apartment building lying on its side. Except it was white and it floated.

"That's the same ship Nan went away on," Jasper said.

"Similar," Mom said. "Read the letter."

Dear Jasper,

Sorry for jumping ship so fast! I saw an opportunity, and I didn't want to miss it. That's the kind of mouse I am. Tricky! I'm having a great time on the cruise. Ten different restaurants! All of them have cheese on the menu. Great for fighting sharks. I'll keep in touch and let you know where I end up next.

Your friend, MM

"MM?" Jasper said. "Is this from Marcel Mouse?"

"Look at the address."

Jasper read: trickymouse@gomail.com.

He jumped up and shouted, "Hurray! We found Marcel!"

Chapter 10

After Jasper read Marcel Mouse's message and ate his snack, he went across the alley and one house down. Ori answered the door and Jasper burst in with his news.

"Marcel Mouse sent me an email! He isn't lost anymore!"

Ori's mom popped her head out of the Watermelon's room. "Jasper," she whispered, "I just got Rachel to sleep. How about you two play outside?"

"I was just going to ask if we could do that,"
Ori said.

Ori and Jasper went out the back door. Jasper
said, "Marcel's on a cruise to Alaska, just like Nan."

"I wonder if he'll see icebergs," Ori said.

Jasper followed Ori into the garage. That was
where Ori had hidden the game that bleeped.

"Do you think a mouse really could send an
email?" Jasper asked.

"If it jumped hard on the keys it could," Ori said.

"A plastic mouse, I mean," Jasper said.

Ori turned on the game. It chimed its tune and
bleeped and Ori quickly turned it off. "If my mom
comes out to check on us, she'll hear it."

Jasper said, "I'll sing the Marcel Mouse song. Then
she won't hear the game."

He stood in the garage doorway and sang at the top of his lungs while Ori played the game inside. The whole time he was singing, Jasper was wishing that the email from Marcel was real. Then Ori's mom opened the back door and told Jasper he was singing too loudly.

"Maybe we'll go over to my house," Jasper said to her.

"That's a great idea," Ori's mom said.

Ori came out of the garage. Ori's mom didn't notice the lump under his shirt that could have been a small, rectangular watermelon, but wasn't. She waved good-bye to them.

"Let's go the long way," Jasper said.

"Why?" Ori asked.

"I'm not allowed to play games that bleep either.

Also, have you ever seen inside our garage? There is so much stuff in there."

They set off walking the long way around the block. Ori pulled the game out of his shirt.

Ori was good at the game now, much better than he was at swinging Marcel Mouse on the so so long string. Thinking about Marcel swinging made Jasper feel all watery again. Then he remembered Marcel was on a cruise. He'd be back, just like Nan had come back from her cruise.

If it really was Marcel writing, and not Mom pretending to be Marcel.

"*Bleep! Bleep! Bleep!*" went the game.

At the end of the block, they turned the corner. Jasper asked to play.

"I thought you didn't want to play," Ori said.

"I didn't want to when I had a mouse to play with. But Marcel's on a cruise now."

Ori wanted to finish his game first.

"*Bleep! Bleep! Bleep!*" went the game.

Ori was so good at playing now that finishing a game took a long time. He could even walk and turn corners while he played. When they needed to cross the street, Jasper tapped his shoulder. Ori stopped walking, but didn't stop playing, while Jasper looked both ways.

"*Bleep! Bleep! Bleep!*"

Finally, Ori finished and handed it over. Jasper asked, "So how do I play?"

They walked along, Ori teaching Jasper. "Press this button."

"*Bleep!*"

"Now pick the game you want."

Jasper picked AstroBunny. The game went *"Bleep!"*

Jasper couldn't walk and play as well as Ori. He lost the first game right away. He asked for another turn and Ori let him play again.

"Bleep! Bleep! Bleep! Bleep! Bleep!"

When he lost the second game and asked for another turn, Ori stopped walking.

"Where are we?" he asked.

Jasper looked around where they were standing. None of the houses were familiar. In one front yard, a swing hung from a tree. He was pretty sure if he had ever seen that house, he would have remembered it. He would have wanted to sneak a ride on the swing.

They walked to the corner and read the street sign.

"I've never heard of Larch Street," Ori said.

"Me neither," said Jasper.

Ori's eyes filled with tears. "We're lost!" he wailed. "We're lost!"

Jasper felt watery, too, and his heart sped up in his chest.

Lost! Lost!

The game interrupted his panic. "*Bleep! Bleep! Bleep!*" it said. It wanted Jasper to keep playing. When Jasper turned it off, his heart slowed down.

He patted Ori on the back to calm him. "What does your mom tell you to do if you ever get lost?"

Ori sniffed. "She says to wait where I am until she finds me."

"That's what my mom told me, too. So that's what we should do," Jasper said.

"But she's never going to find me! She thinks I'm at your house!"

Jasper thought of Marcel Mouse getting flushed down the toilet. Marcel Mouse whooshing through sewer pipes. Wheee! Marcel Mouse arriving at the sewage treatment plant, that so so big concrete building. Marcel had never been there before, but he wasn't afraid.

"Every day Marcel Mouse gets in trouble," Jasper told Ori. "Every day he gets out again."

Ori stopped wailing. He wiped his tears on his sleeve. "How?"

"Like this," Jasper said.

Jasper got down on the grass with his arms folded behind his head and one leg crossed over the other, his toes tapping the air. He looked just like he was sunning himself in a lawn chair. Ori did the same. They both began humming the Marcel Mouse song.

For a long time they lay there, tapping the air with their toes and humming. Jasper waited for some ideas. If he waited long enough, one or two usually came along.

Some clouds floated across the sky. "They look like icebergs," Ori said.

"Marcel's in Alaska," Jasper said. "At least, I think he is."

"The thing is, I already know that," Ori said.

A few minutes later, a big brown dog came along. It loped over and sniffed Jasper and Ori. They sat up in the grass before it could lick their faces.

"No kisses, Baxter," said the man who was walking the dog.

Now Jasper knew the dog's name. If he knew his name, the dog wasn't a stranger anymore. Jasper wasn't supposed to talk to strangers, but nobody had ever told him not to talk to dogs.

"Are you going for a walk, Baxter?" Jasper asked.

"Yes," Baxter's owner said. "Every day we walk to the school and back."

Jasper was starting to feel more confident, just like Marcel. "What school?" he asked Baxter.

The man named the school.

"That's our school!" Ori said.

"The one four blocks that way?" the man asked, pointing.

Jasper and Ori leapt to their feet. They sang the Marcel Mouse song and did the dance, waving high and low and turning in a circle. They weren't lost anymore! Jasper lived the closest to the school, one block away. Ori lived the second closest, across the alley and one house down from Jasper. Hurray!

Baxter barked and danced with them.

Chapter 11

Dear Jasper,

I caught a ride on an iceberg partway to Japan.
Then I rode a current the rest of the way. Tricky!
But don't you try it. I can do it because I float.
I hope you're having fun!

Your friend, MM

This time, Marcel Mouse had sent a picture of himself standing under a pink cherry tree.

"I wonder if Marcel has seen any of those funny toilets," Jasper asked Mom and Dad at supper that night.

Mom and Dad's mouths got small like they were sucking on a peppermint. They glanced at each other and smiled.

"I bet he did see those toilets," Dad said.

"Hmm," Jasper said, looking from Mom to Dad.

Their faces got very straight and serious then, like they'd ironed them. They both looked down at their plates.

"Then why doesn't he hop in the toilet and get flushed back into the ocean? Why doesn't he come home?" Jasper asked.

"That's probably what he's going to do," Dad said.

Mom frowned at Dad. "But he might not come home."

"Why not?" Jasper asked.

"Well …" Mom said.

She scooped some more mashed potatoes onto her plate even though she hadn't finished the potatoes that were already there. She scooped more onto Dad's plate, too. It seemed to Jasper that she was waiting for some ideas to come along.

"Marcel is a traveling mouse. After being stuck in that box for so many years, he just wants to roam."

Dad nodded.

"Where's Marcel going next?" Jasper asked.

Dad said, "If he rides the ocean currents? Australia, I think."

"Why can't he find Uncle Tom and come back for Nan's birthday party? Just for a visit."

Mom and Dad glanced at each other, but they didn't smile.

After supper, Jasper wrote back to Marcel.

Dear Marcel,

My Uncle Tom lives in Australea. He is coming hear for Nans surprise birthday party next week. Can you come home for a visit in Toms sootcase? Then if you want I'll flush you back down the toilet.

At the bottom of the message, Jasper copied out Uncle Tom's address that Mom had given him.

Mom read his message. "Now, Jasper," she said, "maybe Marcel Mouse won't come back with Uncle Tom."

"I know," Jasper said. "But I hope he does."

"But if he doesn't? If he can't? You won't be too disappointed?"

"I'll be so so so so disappointed," Jasper said.

Chapter 12

At school, Ori, Leon, Jasper and Paul C. gave up on hide-and-seek and treasure hunters. It was boring now that they had the so so fun game that bleeped. At recess and lunch they sat in a circle behind the bushes at the back of the schoolyard where the playground monitor couldn't see them. They didn't worry about the girls. The girls were busy with the toy soldiers. They had brought different-colored nail polish and were painting them.

Ori was the best player. He had the highest score.

At first they had a rule that you played until you lost a game. Soon that became boring for everybody except Ori because Ori never lost. So they changed the rule. You could only play for five minutes.

"*Bleep, bleep, bleep, bleep, bleep!*"

"*Bleep, bleep, bleep, bleep, bleep!*"

The monitor was too far away to hear the game bleep for every point Ori scored. But somebody else heard the game. A Grade Six kid in a black hoodie heard and popped up on the other side of the bushes.

"Hey!" he roared. "Who stole my game?"

The game was in Ori's hand. Even if he hadn't been taking his turn, the Grade Six kid would have known Ori had taken it. He would have known because Leon pointed right at Ori and said, "He stole it!"

The Grade Six kid snatched the game out of Ori's hands. Ori said in a tiny, terrified voice, "I-I-I didn't steal it. I was only borrowing it."

The bell rang. The Grade Six kid in the black hoodie told Ori, "I'll see you at lunch."

Leon and Paul C. waited until he had swaggered off. Then they ran back into the school so they wouldn't get the lates.

Ori didn't run. He was shaking with fear. Jasper walked slowly beside him.

"I'm in trouble," Ori said.

"Every day Marcel Mouse gets in trouble. Every day he gets out again," Jasper reminded him.

"The thing is?" Ori said. "Marcel Mouse is just a toy. I'll probably go to jail."

Jasper stopped walking and stared at Ori, his good

friend and neighbor who lived across the alley and one house down.

He said, "I won't let them take you."

When the bell rang for lunch, Ori was afraid to leave the classroom. Ms. Tosh had to shoo him and Jasper out. They got their lunch boxes. Ori dragged his feet down the hall toward the lunchroom. His shoulders slumped and his head hung low.

They didn't speak. Jasper watched for the Grade Six kid in the black hoodie. Then, as they passed the Lost and Found box, both of them looked at it.

Jasper said, "Get in."

Nobody paid any attention to Jasper sitting on the Lost and Found box, swinging his legs and humming the Marcel Mouse song while he ate his lunch. Nobody noticed that he seemed to be talking to himself.

"Everything okay in there?" Jasper said to nobody. "If I see him, I'll kick the box three times."

Mrs. Jamil and Mrs. Kinoshita must have been in a meeting. Nobody told him to go outside and play.

After Jasper finished eating, he lay on the box with his arms folded behind his head and one leg crossed over the other, his toes tapping the air.

"Still nobody around," he said.

He waited for an idea to come along, an idea about what Ori should do. While he waited, he watched for the Grade Six kid in the black hoodie.

"And the police," Ori said from inside the box.

"Tell me if you see the police."

"What if I do see the police?" Jasper asked.

"I'm going to turn myself in. I'm not very comfortable in here. Jail is probably better."

"Marcel Mouse was in Nan's storage room for years and years," Jasper said.

Ori groaned.

By the time the after-lunch bell rang, Jasper had a plan. He sat up on the Lost and Found box.

"Dress up in the Lost clothes!"

"What?" said Ori, inside the box. "Why?"

"For a disguise!"

"Won't he remember my face?"

"Borrow Paul C.'s glasses."

Just then the Grade Six kid came strolling down the hall. Jasper kicked the side of the box three times.

The kid came right over. "I didn't see your friend at lunch."

"He went home," Jasper lied.

"Move," he said.

Jasper sat tight on the Lost and Found box, clutching the lid.

"Move it." The Grade Six kid pulled the game that bleeped out of the pocket of his hoodie. "I have to put this back."

"Isn't it yours?" Jasper asked.

"Not exactly. Tell your friend to put it back after he's used it. We have to take turns, right?"

"Right," Jasper said.

The kid handed over the game that bleeped. "Stick it all the way down at the bottom or everybody will be using it."

"Okay," Jasper said.

The kid held up his palm so Jasper could give him a high-five. Then he strolled away.

As soon as he was gone, Jasper slid off the box and opened the lid. Ori blinked up at the light.

"Did you hear what he said?" Jasper asked. "You can still borrow it!"

Ori stood up in the box. "I never want to see that game again!"

Chapter 13

Just before Jasper and Dad left to pick up Uncle Tom from the airport, a new message came from Marcel Mouse. Mom called for Jasper to read it.

Look at me, Jasper! This is fun! I'm going to stay here for a while! I'll write soon!

The picture showed Marcel in the pouch of a kangaroo.

In the car Dad said to Jasper, "It sounds like Marcel

Mouse won't be coming home with Uncle Tom. That's too bad. But it's great he's having a lot of fun."

Jasper said, "The most fun he has is when I make him swing at the end of the so so long string around my neck."

Dad turned to look at Jasper in the backseat. "I'm sorry about Marcel, Jasper. I really am."

"Me, too," Jasper said, and sniffed.

Marcel wasn't ever coming back.

At the airport, they had to wait a long time for Uncle Tom to come through the sliding glass door. Jasper recognized him first. He looked a lot like Dad except his hair was lighter and he had a little beard. When he saw Jasper jumping up and down and waving beside Dad, Uncle Tom let go of his suitcase and ran for them. He hugged Jasper and lifted him in the air.

"He's *my* little boy!" Uncle Tom told Dad. Then he started to run away with Jasper in his arms.

Dad chased after them, calling, "No, he's mine! Give him back!"

Everybody stared. Jasper laughed and laughed.

Finally, Uncle Tom stopped, still holding Jasper tight.

"What will you give me for him?"

"My dessert tonight," Dad said.

Uncle Tom looked at Jasper, trying to decide if it was a fair trade. "Nope," he told Dad. "I'm keeping him!"

That was when a scary security guard marched over. Uncle Tom set Jasper back on the ground and hurried to get his suitcase. In an airport, you're not allowed to leave your suitcase even for a minute. And you're not allowed to steal other people's kids.

The whole way home in the car, Jasper kept

crowing, "You almost went to jail, Uncle Tom! You almost went to jail!"

At home, Jasper sat on the bed in the spare room watching Uncle Tom unpack his suitcase. The suitcase was half full of presents, mostly for Nan. But one small present was for Jasper. It fit in the palm of his hand.

Jasper looked at the package. It was just about the size of a little orange mouse with big ears and big feet. His mouth fell open for a second. He jumped up and gave Uncle Tom a hug.

Jasper tore off the paper.

Inside was a furry little koala bear.

"Check this out, Jasper." Uncle Tom showed him how squeezing the koala's shoulders would make its arms open. That way the koala could clip on to his clothes.

"Thank you," Jasper said. He hoped Uncle Tom couldn't see how watery he felt.

After Uncle Tom had finished unpacking, supper was ready. Jasper brought the little koala to the table and showed Mom and Dad how he clipped on to things. He left him clipped to his shirtsleeve.

"That's great," Dad said. "Let's hope he doesn't unclip and fall you-know-where."

"Don't you fall in the toilet like Marcel Mouse," Jasper told the koala.

Uncle Tom sat up straight in his chair. "Marcel Mouse?" He sprang to his feet. "*Marcel Mouse! Marcel Mouse! A mouse who's lots of fun! Marcel Mouse! Marcel Mouse! He's a tricky one!*" He waved his hands high. He waved them low.

Dad got up and joined him, turning in a circle and

waving his hands and singing. So did Jasper. Mom
stayed at the table, watching them and laughing.

"He was *my* mouse! *Mine!*"

"I traded for him," Dad shouted back.

"You took him!" Uncle Tom shouted at Dad.
"Now you have to give me this little boy!" Uncle
Tom snatched up Jasper again.

That's how Jasper could tell they were just pretending to be mad at each other. That, and everybody was laughing.

When they were all sitting back down at the table, Tom said, "What about Marcel Mouse?"

Mom said, "Jasper? Do you want to tell Uncle Tom what happened?"

Jasper did. He told Uncle Tom how Nan had found the box of toys in her storage room and given it to Jasper. How, as soon as Jasper saw Marcel, he never took him off except at school and in bed. "Because it's Very Dangerous to wear a so so long string around your neck when you're asleep. You could strangle."

Uncle Tom nodded.

Jasper told him how the lid of the toilet fell and snapped the string.

"No!" Uncle Tom said.

Jasper told him about the sewage treatment plant and how no matter how much water you pour in the toilet, the water level stays the same.

"Really?" Uncle Tom said.

And he told about the emails Marcel was sending and how he was in Australia now.

"Now?" Uncle Tom said.

Jasper nodded.

"I'll tell you what, Jasper. When I get back to Australia, I'm going to do my best to find him. In the meantime, I hope that koala makes you feel a little bit better."

The koala did make him feel a little better, and so did talking about Marcel. Jasper smiled at everybody around the table and patted Koala, who was hanging on to his shirtsleeve.

Chapter 14

The next day, the day of the surprise party, was so so so so busy. Jasper helped clean the house and put up the decorations. He blew up so many balloons he thought his head would blow off.

Dad cooked and Mom cooked. Uncle Tom took a long nap because in Australia it was already tomorrow, which Jasper didn't understand. Nan phoned and asked Mom if she wanted to go shopping, and Mom told a Big Lie while Jasper rolled around on the floor trying not to laugh.

"David will pick you up at the same time for dinner," Mom said. "I made a cake for your birthday."

"Why did you tell her about the cake?" Jasper asked after she hung up.

"She knows we'd never forget her birthday. But she'll be so surprised to find the house full of friends."

"She'll be so so so surprised to see Uncle Tom!" Jasper said.

"That's the idea," Mom said.

After Uncle Tom woke up from his nap, Mom and Dad made him get out of the house. "You're just in the way now. Go for a walk with Jasper."

So Jasper and Uncle Tom set out walking. Koala went, too, hanging on to Jasper's sleeve.

"This is my favorite thing to do when I'm in a new place, Jasper."

"What?" Jasper asked.

"Walking around until I get lost."

Jasper said, "If you want to get lost, I know a good place. I got lost there a few days ago with Ori."

They walked and turned corners and crossed streets. All the way, Uncle Tom entertained Jasper with stories about the terrible things Dad had done to him when they were kids.

"He painted my toy soldiers with nail polish!" Tom said.

"I know," Jasper said. "They were in the box of toys Nan found."

"Really?" Uncle Tom said. "I'd like them back."

"Oh," Jasper said. "I don't have them anymore. I …"

Before Jasper could explain what had happened to the soldiers, Uncle Tom pointed to a sign on a post:

GIANT YARD SALE.

"That's another thing I love. Other people's junk."

Jasper and Uncle Tom followed the arrow on the sign. In the next block, tables were set out on the front lawns of all the houses. One of them was the house with the tree swing.

"Are you lost yet?" Jasper asked.

Uncle Tom laughed. He bought Jasper lemonade from the kids at the lemonade stand using Australian money. Jasper tried the tree swing. Then they wandered off to look at the things for sale. Tom looked at the books. Jasper looked at the electronic things. And there on the table was something he knew so so well — a game that bleeped!

He turned it on. It worked!

"*Bleep! Bleep! Bleep!*" went the game.

Uncle Tom came up while Jasper was playing AstroBunny. "Do you want it? I'll buy it for you."

"No thanks." Jasper set it back down.

They walked over to the next table, which was covered with toys — stuffed animals, board games, a tea set. And a box full of little toys. Lots and lots of little toys.

"Look," Jasper told Uncle Tom. "Soldiers."

Uncle Tom picked one out of the box. "We could probably get our hands on some nail polish. Then we could paint them and put them somewhere for your dad to find. Does he take his lunch to work?"

"Yes!"

"He'd be so mad if he opened his lunch box and found —"

"Pink soldiers!" Jasper laughed.

"Help me," Uncle Tom said, and he and Jasper began to pick through the jumble of toys for the soldiers.

Uncle Tom reached in and plucked out something else.

Something orange and made of plastic.

Something with big ears and big feet.

Jasper looked at Uncle Tom and Uncle Tom looked at Jasper.

"Marcel Mouse!" they both yelled.

All the guests arrived for Nan's party. The house was full of friends. There were old friends with gray hair and new friends from her apartment building. Jasper got to carry a tray with all the fancy snacks that Mom had made.

Dad kept shaking his head and telling Jasper, "I can't believe it. I can't believe Marcel found his way back."

Finally, Jasper had to say, "Dad? It's not the *real* Marcel. That's impossible. But I love this Marcel, too."

Dad left to get Nan. Ten minutes later the phone rang, and Mom called over all the voices, "They'll be here in five minutes!"

Everybody stopped talking and sat in silence. Jasper tiptoed around with the tray.

A few minutes later, they heard the car pull up outside. Jasper set down the tray. Two car doors slammed, then footsteps came up the stairs to the porch. Jasper put both hands over his mouth so he wouldn't shout too early.

The door opened and Nan stepped inside. She

looked around the room with so so wide eyes. When she saw Uncle Tom, she put her hand on her heart and took a step back.

Then Jasper, standing to the side so he had enough room, made the orange mouse hanging from the so so long string around his neck swing. Wheee!

"Marcel Mouse!" Nan cried. "You came back for my birthday!"

And everybody shouted out, "*SURPRISE!*"

Praise for
the Jasper John Dooley series

Jasper John Dooley: Star of the Week

★ Best Children's Books of the Year, Bank Street Children's Book Committee

"Well-written, funny, and engaging … Share with kids looking for a boy version of Sara Pennypacker's Clementine series or with fans of Lenore Look's Alvin Ho books." — *Booklist*

Jasper John Dooley: Left Behind

★ Named to *Kirkus Reviews'* Best Books of 2013

★ "So aptly, charmingly and amusingly depicted that it's impossible not to be both captivated and compelled." — *Kirkus Reviews,* starred review

Jasper John Dooley: NOT in Love

★ Named to *Kirkus Reviews'* Best Books of 2014

★ "Adderson perfectly captures the trials of early childhood, and with brief text and a simple vocabulary, she breathes full life into her cast of characters." — *Kirkus Reviews,* starred review

Jasper John Dooley: You're in Trouble

★ "Another highly entertaining and enthusiastic outing in a series that's perfect for readers new to chapter books and as a captivating read-aloud." — *Kirkus Reviews,* starred review